Fritz and the Mess Fairy

∗ R O S E M A R Y   W E L L S ∗

Collins

An Imprint of HarperCollins*Publishers*

First published in the USA in 1991 by
Dial Books for Young Readers -
a division of Penguin Books USA Inc.
First published in the UK in 1992 by
HarperCollins Publishers Ltd.

Copyright © 1991 by Rosemary Wells
Design by Jane Byers Bierhorst

ISBN 0 00 193641-7

The artwork for each picture is
a watercolour painting on paper.

Printed and bound in Hong Kong

For the new Phyllis

"Have you cleaned up your room yet, Fritz?"
asked Fritz's mother.
"I will!" shouted Fritz.

Fritz stuffed a month's laundry, twelve heaps of old
sweets, half a dozen wet towels, six silver ice cream
spoons stuck to six dessert plates, three library books
with ice lolly stick bookmarks, and a peanut butter
and jam sandwich all under his bed.
"Suppertime!" yelled Fritz's sister, Tiffany.

"Fritz," asked Fritz's mother,
"have you seen my silver ice cream spoons?"
"Somebody must have taken them," said Fritz.
"Not me," said Tiffany. "I don't eat ice cream
because I'm on a diet."

"Drink your milk, Fritz," said Fritz's father.
Fritz put a dab of relish in his milk
so that it would turn a weird colour.
"Something's wrong with it," said Fritz.

Everybody had finished eating and had left the table by
the time Fritz had removed all the raisins from his toast,
separated all the peas out of his soup, and slipped most of
his potatoes under his seat cushion.
"It's your turn to do the dishes tonight, Fritz,"
said Fritz's mother.
"I will!" said Fritz.

But just as Fritz was about to start washing up,
he remembered his science project was
due the very next day.

Quickly Fritz chose an experiment from the back of the book.

It required a raw egg, a feather, copper wire, rose water glycerine, and a junior rocket booster.

Fritz assembled everything but the rose water, which was on Tiffany's dressing table.

As soon as Tiffany went out with her friends,
Fritz tiptoed into her room to borrow just a little bit.

But Fritz could not get the science experiment to work.
He tried again and again, using even more eggs,
coils of copper wire, a bolster full of feathers, and
nearly the whole bottle of rose water glycerine.

Suddenly his bedroom door opened.

"Your name is mud in my book, Son," grumbled his father.

"My copper wire's all gone and my toolbox is a mess!"

"Fritz," intoned his mother, "the kitchen is a shambles because of you!"

Tiffany squealed, "You're in hot water with me, Birdbrain."

"I didn't do it!" yelled Fritz, and he slammed his door.

and threw all his lorries out of the window into the flower garden.

Fritz was too sleepy to clean up.
Outside his window the night air stirred softly
through the willow branches. Moonlight slid between
the shadows and an owl flew over. But as the hours passed
and midnight went by, something strange began taking place
in the beaker on the floor of Fritz's room.

It was a once-in-a-lifetime chemical change.
The molecules of the rose water began to crystallize in the
egg white. Soon the process got out of control. This heated
up the copper wire. As a result the rocket booster burst
into overtime action. The tail pipes emitted noxious gases.

The smell woke Fritz.
"What's that?" he asked.

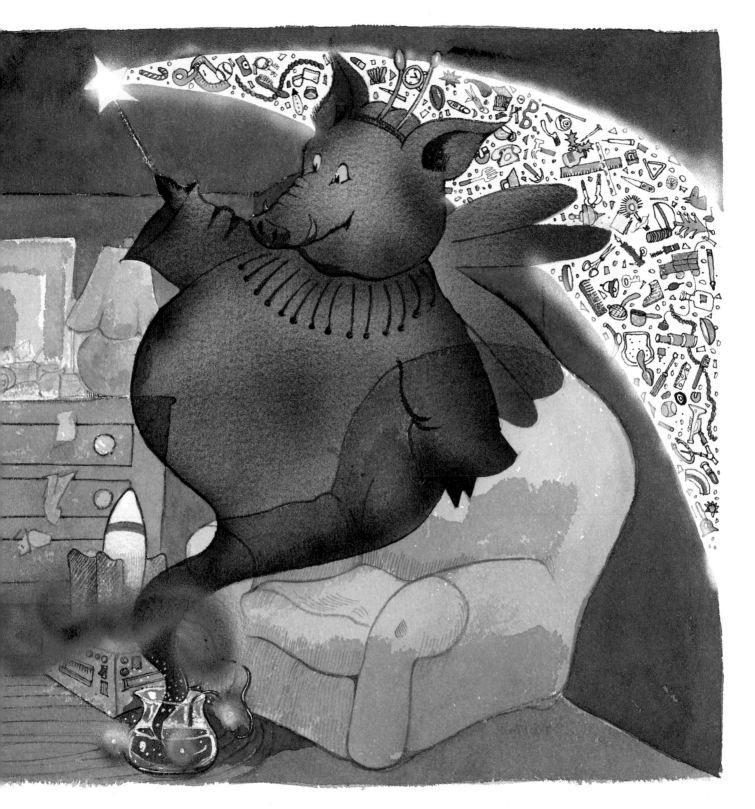

"It's me!" sang the Mess Fairy.
"What are you going to do?" asked Fritz.
"You'll see," answered the Mess Fairy.

The Mess Fairy rolled up her sleeves.
Then she took all the socks out of Fritz's drawer
and hurled them around the room.

In the bathroom she squeezed
the toothpaste out of the
wrong end of the tube.

In the kitchen she drank
lemonade out of twenty-three
different glasses.

And in the den she shuffled
six packs of cards together and
mixed up the pieces from ten
different board games.

Soon the living room was a snarl of interconnected
extension cords. Fritz began to cry.
"Do something!" he said to himself.

"What can I do against her? She's so overpowering!"
he answered himself.
Suddenly Fritz had an idea.

While the Mess Fairy was busy with the lamps, Fritz quietly reassembled his experiment, feathers and rose glycerine, eggs and copper wire. But this time he put the rocket booster's motor into reverse.

Once again the molecules crystallized and the wire
overheated. But now the rocket's engines sucked the air in
the room into a whirling funnel, creating a peculiar
black hole. The Mess Fairy was swallowed right up, leaving
only a lingering fragrance of pine needles.

Fritz jumped into his mother and father's bed.
"Did you have a bad dream, my little carrot cake?"
whispered his mother.
"We love you, Son," murmured his father.

Fritz was ashamed.
He felt terrible about leaving the dirty kitchen for his
hardworking mother to clean.
He was mortified when he remembered his father's toolbox.
And he could have kicked himself for spilling Tiffany's
nail polish and lotions all over her rug.
Fritz resolved to clean up the whole house.

He coiled up all the extension cords and put them in the right drawer. He sorted the cards and game pieces, scrubbed up the toothpaste, put his toys on his shelves, put his rubbish in the bin, and hauled his laundry to the washing machine.

He washed up the dessert plates and the ice cream spoons
and the dishes left from the night before and all
twenty-three lemonade glasses.

A shaft of morning light greeted the sparkling house.
Fritz rested at last. He felt good and clean and neat.

"I love them so," he said, "I'm going to make them
their favourite breakfasts-in-bed!"
And he did.
Fritz made bran muffins with orange slices for his father,

buttermilk pancakes for his mother, and special
diet waffles for Tiffany. Fritz was so proud...

"It's the new Fritz," he said.